D1451970

TURTLE ROCKS

Written by Audrey Galex

Illustrated by Colleen Finn

It's fun to walk in the forest! Leaves vibrating in the breeze welcome you with polite applause. Wonders are all around you. You might even find some treasures under the trees! Maybe you'll spot a turtle walking along the path. Where could it be going? Let's find out. Together!

The journey that gave birth to this book is also a story of traveling together toward a destination, and the author is eternally grateful to all who joined her. Many thanks to illustrator Colleen Finn for patient guidance and delightful images. Thanks to life coach and friend Liz Hanzi for her wise counsel, encouragement, and accountability check-ins. Thank you to author Stephanie Moore for asking a question that "cracked open the story." Thanks to artist Miriam Karp, keeper of turtles, who reminded the author that turtles are aquatic. Thanks to Lisa McClure Guthrie for copy-editing and finding the stream in the forest. Gratitude to Eyal Schechter for tweaking the text to tell a bigger story and thank you to Dave Schechter for enduring the writing of this story in its many permutations. Thanks to so many others whose names aren't mentioned but whose love, encouragement, and suggestions made all the difference in turning this dream into reality.

Dedicated to

Dave, Maayan, Eyal and Ronen

Once upon a time, there was a pond.

Across the pond lay a log.

On that log lounged a line of tiny turtles.

The turtles sunned themselves on that log every afternoon.

One dewy morning, a tiny turtle walked along a forest path toward that pond. One webbed foot followed another.

He came upon a rock just slightly bigger than himself.

Seeing the rock blocking his way made him angry.

"How will I ever get to the log with that rock in my way? All the other turtles will be at the pond. I'm going to WAIT for somebody ELSE to move the rock!"

So, he pulled in his head, tucked in his legs, and waited.

And he waited and waited and waited so long that the dust and the dirt covered him up and he looked like a rock.

The next morning another tiny turtle walked along the same forest path toward the pond. One webbed foot followed another.

She came upon a rock just slightly bigger than herself.

She longed to sun herself on the log laying across the pond alongside her turtle friends.

Seeing the rock blocking her way made her sad.

"Oh ME, oh MY. Why does this always happen to me? I can't even see the pond! How do I know it's still there? I'm going to WAIT for somebody ELSE to move the rock."

So, she pulled in her head, tucked in her legs, and waited.

And she waited and waited and waited so long that the dust and the dirt covered her up and she looked like a rock.

The next morning another tiny turtle walked along the same forest path toward the pond. One webbed foot followed another.

It came upon a rock just slightly bigger than itself.

It longed to sun itself on the log that lay across the pond, alongside its turtle friends. It longed to watch dragonflies dart between lily pads. It couldn't wait to see fish splash in the shallow water.

Seeing the rock made it curious.

"I wonder what that rock is doing here? Maybe it's a marker telling me the pond is straight ahead!"

So, it stretched out its head, straightened its legs, and walked around the rock.

But something strange began to happen. The rock began to tremble. The rock began to shake.

The rock shook and trembled and shook so hard that the dirt fell off and a turtle emerged.

"Are you here to move the rock?" asked the turtle who had been too sad to walk to the pond.

"No," said the curious turtle. "I'm going to the pond to sun myself on a log. Will you come with me?"

"I'd like to but how do you know the pond is still there? You can't even see it!"

"I don't know for sure," said the curious turtle, "but if I keep moving forward, I'm bound to find out!"

The sad turtle began to follow the curious turtle.

But another rock blocked their path.

That made the curious turtle even more curious.

So, it stretched out its head, straightened its legs, and walked over the rock. The sad turtle followed.

But something strange began to happen. The rock began to tremble. The rock began to shake.

The rock shook and trembled and shook so hard that the dirt fell off and a turtle emerged.

"Ouch! Unless you're going to move that rock, you'd better get off my back!" demanded the angry turtle.

"I'm sorry," said the curious turtle. "I didn't mean to hurt you. You looked like a rock. We're going to the pond. Would you like to come with us?"

"What about that rock in the path?" The angry turtle tilted his head toward the rock.

"Don't worry. We'll find a way around it. Together!"

The curious turtle took a step and then stopped.

It looked at the sad turtle and said:

"My family and my teachers taught me that there would be rocks in my path but don't let that stop you! Turn those rocks into stepping stones!"

When the sad turtle heard those words, she felt a tug of happiness.

The curious turtle turned to the angry turtle and said:

"I crawled around one rock and climbed over another. I started this journey alone and now I have friends. Together, we can push this rock out of the way and get to the pond!""

When the angry turtle heard those words, he felt a tug of courage.

"OK. I'll help," he said. "It's worth a try."

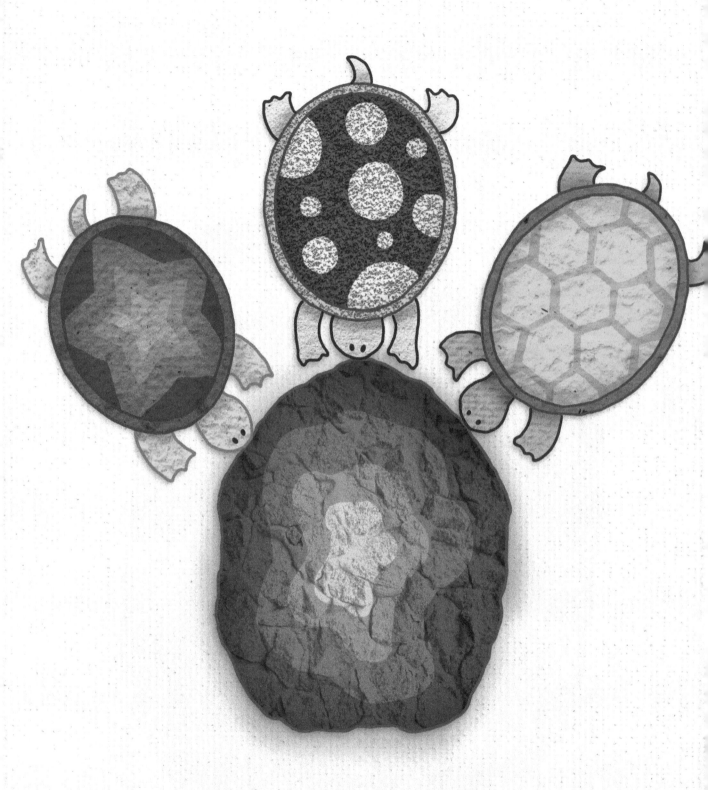

They knew this was going to be hard, so they stretched out their heads, straightened their legs, and pressed against the rock.

But something strange began to happen. The rock began to tremble, the rock began to shake. When the rock turned over, the dirt fell off and another turtle emerged!

"Oh my! I must have fallen asleep. Thanks for waking me up! I was on my way to the pond, but it felt too far to go alone so I gave up. If you're going to the pond,

I'd like to join you."

The happy turtle was even happier than before.

The courageous turtle felt even more courageous.

The turtle that had given up felt a burst of energy.

And the curious turtle felt confident they could get to the pond together!

"We're ready to go to the pond!"

As the new friends began to move forward, they heard a twig snap.

Looking back, they saw that the courageous turtle had turned off the path.

"I don't want to go to the pond," he admitted. "I guess I was only going because everyone told me I should. I really like the stream in the shady forest and not the pond in the hot afternoon sun."

With a wave of his webbed foot to say goodbye to his new friends, he pushed out his head, straightened his legs, and walked into the underbrush.

"Good luck!" called the curious turtle. It wondered what new trails the courageous turtle would create.

Overjoyed, the other turtles found their way to the pond.

One of the tiny turtles jumped into the water
for a swim.

The others found their place on the log.

And that's where they stretched out their heads, straightened their legs, and lounged for the rest of the day, in the warmth of the afternoon sun.

EPILOGUE

The next time you find a turtle in the forest, he might be a turtle that turned his anger into courage, followed his dream, and created a new path.

When you see a turtle swimming, it might be a turtle that didn't think it could get to the pond alone.

When you see turtles sunning themselves on a log, one might be a turtle who was sad and became happy when another turtle invited her to come along.

And one of them might be the one with curiosity and a can-do attitude that helped the others discover that what sometimes begins as a long, lonely adventure alone can become a story of friendship, as well as a tale of finding your inner strength, discovering your unique path, and together, overcoming once seemingly insurmountable obstacles, often no bigger than yourself.

ABOUT THE AUTHOR

Audrey Galex loves to walk in forests, and just about anywhere else, because there's always a chance of finding a story around the next bend. She's produced television programs, told stories on stage and in workshops, and helped others record their stories to connect communities and generations. Audrey can often be found on a dance floor, in a coffee shop, playing miniature golf, or photographing discarded mattresses. She and her husband, journalist Dave Schechter, have three adult children and two grand dogs, and live in Atlanta.

Turtle Rocks is her first book.